Serena and
the Wild Doll

Serena and the Wild Doll

written by Philip Coristine

art by Julia Gukova

Annick Press Ltd.

Toronto • New York • Vancouver

We acknowledge the support of the Canada Council for the Arts, the Ontario Arts Council, and the Government of Canada through the Book Publishing Industry Development Program (BPIDP) for our publishing activities.

Cataloging in Publication Data

Coristine, Philip
    Serena and the wild doll

ISBN 1-55037-649-7 (bound) ISBN 1-55037-648-9 (pbk.)

I. Gukova, Julia, II. Title.

PS8555.O625S47 2000 jC813'.6 C00-930586-6
PZ7.C8158Se 2000

The art in this book was rendered in mixed media.
The text was typeset in Giovanni.

Distributed in Canada by:
Firefly Books Ltd.
3680 Victoria Park Avenue
Willowdale, ON
M2H 3K1

Published in the U.S.A. by Annick Press (U.S.) Ltd.
Distributed in the U.S.A. by:
Firefly Books (U.S.) Inc.
P.O. Box 1338
Ellicott Station
Buffalo, NY 14205

Printed and bound in Canada by Friesens, Altona, Manitoba.

visit us at: **www.annickpress.com**

For Naomi
P.C.

For Alyosha
J.G.

Little Miss Muffet
sat on a tuffet
eating her curds and whey,
along came a spider . . .

There once was a doll who was stored in an attic full of musty old storybooks and other forgotten things. The children she loved had grown up and left home, but Serena still listened for their footsteps on the stairs. She dusted herself every morning, combed her hair, and sat, smiling hopefully, but no one came.

There was one window.
If she stood close, Serena could see a tree.
"Come! Come!" the crows called.
"Thank you for inviting me," Serena
would say. But she never went out to play.
All day long now, she stared into a
mirror, fretting about her fading
paint and fussing with her hair.
"Another cup of tea?" she
would whisper to the mirror.
And the face in the
mirror would whisper
back, "Thank you. And
another cookie, please."
She forgot all about
the world outside. The
birds fell silent, then
flew away.
The years went by.
No one came.

Suddenly, one afternoon, Serena finally heard the sound of small footsteps on the stairs.

"They've come at last!" she whispered. "I knew they would some-day!" She sat up straight and posed.

The door swung open. A fragrance of the woods just after the rain and of sunshine filled the attic.

The visitor tiptoed in. But it wasn't a child after all. It was a ragged and grimy doll.

Serena was disappointed. "Who are you?" she cried. "How did you get in here?"

"I'm a wild doll, Serena," the visitor said, with a voice like the wind when it whispers through the trees. "The world is beautiful. Come out and play."

Serena shook her head. "I'm expecting the children this afternoon for tea," she said. "Go away. You'll frighten them."

And soon Serena was alone again.

The fragrance of the woods still filled the room, and the wild doll's words echoed softly: The world is beautiful. Come out and play.

Serena sat for a long time, wondering if it were true. She stood on her tiptoes, looking out over the rooftops.

A green star beckoned in the evening sky.

She suddenly turned around and started down the stairs, past the kitchen, past the children's room. How it had changed! No one was home. And for the first time ever, Serena went out into the world.

At first all she saw were boots and
horses' hooves and carriage wheels
rushing by. She was knocked to the
ground and stepped on by mistake.
She was frightened and looked for a
hiding place, but no one took notice
of her. No one had time.

For hours she wandered down dark
alleys, searching for the wild doll.

And then the moon came out from behind a cloud and bathed the world in light. Suddenly Serena saw a fierce animal coming towards her through the shadows. She hid behind a tree, but the fox kept coming, growling and grumbling hungrily.

Just then, a soft voice said, "Don't worry. He won't hurt you. He's hungry. We should feed him." It was the wild doll. She had some berries and gave them to Serena.

"Do foxes like these?" Serena asked.

"Let's see."

Serena stood still, holding out the berries. The fox came creeping up and sniffed at her hand.

"He's an old friend," the wild doll said, gently stroking his fur.

Serena and the wild doll climbed on
the fox's back and he took them for a
ride. The wild doll showed Serena
beautiful places. There were gardens
fragrant with flowers and houses
warm with lights and a rushing
river—and even a fountain in a park.

Later they crept into a fairgrounds, dark and silent, but Serena found a switch to the giant Ferris wheel and turned it on. Quickly they scrambled into the lowest cabin, holding onto the fox. Slowly, majestically, the giant wheel began to move.

"Why are you wild?" Serena asked after a few moments. "Don't you belong to a family?"

"I used to, a long time ago," the wild doll replied. "Then one Sunday afternoon we all went on a trip and I fell from the carriage without anyone noticing. I'm sure they came looking for me. But it had been such a long ride . . ."

Serena sighed. "Oh, how sad," she said.

"I'm not sad," said the wild doll. "The whole wide world is my home now. All the wild animals are my friends."

Serena said nothing. I wonder if I can be wild too, she thought.

That very moment the night watchman woke up. "Someone is playing on the Ferris wheel again!" he shouted, stomping outside.

The fox sprang down from his perch, with the delighted dolls hanging on for dear life.

The fox was swift and strong. Soon they were safe. The dolls said goodbye to him, and thank you, and went on their own back into the sleeping town.

They peeked in the window of the dollmaker's shop and saw the old man still working at his bench with gentle hands.

"I remember you now," Serena said, turning to look at the wild doll. "We are sisters, you and I."

The dollmaker heard a tapping on the window. When he went to look, there was no one there, but he found wildflowers on the windowsill.

Presently, the birds began to sing to wake the dawn.

"It's time to say goodbye," the wild doll said. "But you know you can come out and play whenever you choose."

"No! Don't leave me!" Serena cried. "Where will I live? What will happen to me?"

"Enjoy yourself. Go where the children go!" said the wild doll, and then she was gone.

The sun began to rise. Serena slipped through the stirring town, amid the sights and sounds of morning.

"Go where the children go," Serena whispered. "I think I know where that might be."

And so she went to a playground and sat on a swing, with the sun on her face.

The children saw her sitting there and, yes, Serena found a happy new home that day. But once in a while, when the green star was calling her, she went out into the night to play.

Other books illustrated
by Julia Gukova:

The Mole's Daughter

Freedom Child of the Sea
by Richardo Keens-Douglas

The Other Side
by Alejandro Aura